Cat in the Clouds

Eric Pinder

Illustrations by
T.B.R. Walsh

Charleston | London

THE
History
PRESS

Published by The History Press
Charleston, SC 29403
www.historypress.net

First published 2009
Second printing 2009
Third printing 2009

Manufactured in Canada

ISBN 978.1.59629.680.0

Library of Congress Cataloging-in-Publication Data

Pinder, Eric, 1970-
Cat in the clouds / Eric Pinder ; illustrations by T.B.R. Walsh.
p. cm.
Includes bibliographical references and index.
ISBN 978-1-59629-680-0 (alk. paper)
1. Mount Washington Observatory--History. 2. Cats--New Hampshire--Washington, Mount--Biography.
3. Washington, Mount (N.H.)--Biography. 4. Cats--New Hampshire--Washington, Mount--History. 5. Cats-
-Climatic factors--New Hampshire--Washington, Mount. 6. Human-animal relationships--New Hampshire--
Washington, Mount. I. Walsh, T. B. R. II. Title.
QC875.U72M6853 2009
551.5072'07421--dc22
2009008967

To Susan, Mark and Nin. Special thanks also to Sarah, Tim and Gus.
  —Eric Pinder

Thank you Eric, for including me in this venture,
and thanks Eek and Zoe for your help body doubling for Nin.
  —T.B.R. Walsh

Since 1932, a handful of hardy meteorologists—and courageous cats—have lived at the Mount Washington Observatory, also known as the "Home of the World's Worst Weather." Heavy snow, freezing fog and record-breaking winds make the summit of New England's highest peak an ideal location for studying the elements.

Nin showed up on the doorstep one day, looking for a place to stay.
He brushed against Mark's legs and jumped right into Susan's lap.
  "We already have two cats," Susan said. Nin just purred and fell asleep.

Nin loved Susan and Mark, but he and the other two cats did not get along. They had to share a dinner bowl. They had to share the sofa. Most of all, they had to share Mark and Susan. There were three cats now, but Mark and Susan still only had two laps. The cats had to take turns sitting, purring and being petted.

Nin wasn't used to sharing. He had always been an only cat.

"Maybe I'll take Nin to Mount Washington," said Mark. Mount Washington is a cold, snowy mountain, but high on the summit you'll find a warm, safe observatory. Only a few people live there. They study the weather. How deep is the snow? How fast does the wind blow? How cloudy is the sky?

Every other week, Mark lived at the observatory high above the clouds. "The mountain can be a lonely place in the winter," he said. "I bet a cat would be welcome there."

It was a damp, gray day when Nin and Mark drove to Mount Washington. Nin couldn't sit still. He tried to hop on Mark's lap. "Not while I'm driving," said Mark. Nin jumped in the back seat and watched as spruce trees, lakes and hills raced by.

They drove out of Vermont and into New Hampshire. Looming in the distance, Nin saw a snowcapped peak: Mount Washington.

It was cold and snowy and blustery at the bottom of Mount Washington.
Nin, Mark and the rest of the crew crowded into the back of a snow tractor.

For hours, the tractor shoved aside towering snowdrifts. Rime covered the windows, so Nin couldn't see outside. Neither could the driver. The fog and blowing snow were too thick. The snow tractor had to stop and wait. The road to the summit curved around the top of a great ravine, and no one wanted to risk falling over the edge.

The snow tractor was a noisy, bumpy, uncomfortable machine. Nin sat in people's laps, but he was not purring anymore. He wanted the trip to end.

At last the fog cleared. A building appeared—the observatory! Everyone jumped out of the cold snow tractor and into the warm building.

Nin wanted to explore this strange new place. Everywhere he found new sights, new smells and new faces. As people unzipped their parkas and pulled off gloves, hats, goggles and scarves, Nin wandered away.
  Where did he go? The crew didn't know.

Nin did not go far. He found a room full of beeping computers and blinking lights. A ladder led up to the ceiling, where one of the tiles was ajar. What was up there? Quick as a flash, Nin bounded up the ladder and through the hole.

Thump, thump, thump. In the next room, Mark and the crew drank hot chocolate and talked about the weather. They heard noises overhead. The ceiling tiles jiggled. "What's that?" said Mark.

"Is that a rat?" someone else asked. Suddenly, Nin peeked down at them. He wanted to join the conversation, too.

Nin liked to watch the meteorologists work.

Every hour they climbed up the tall tower to knock ice off the weather instruments. Nin went, too, as far as he dared. He hopped from step to step all the way up the metal ladder to the Cold Room, right up to the wooden door that led outside. He wouldn't go farther. Beyond that door the wind roared. Chunks of ice hurtled across the sky. Mark and the others had to clear the ice without Nin's help.

When the wind howled, stronger than a hurricane, Nin's new friends played a game. They tried to walk all the way around the observation deck without being swept off their feet. Most fell down. They had to crawl back to the door.

Some sat on sleds and held out their arms like sails. A strong gust pushed them like hockey pucks across the deck. What fun!

Nin stayed safe inside the tower door. He was too small and light to play in the wind.

Nin liked to sit by the windows and watch the
ravens soar. He watched a red fox trot across
the snow. Once he even saw a bear!

On calm days he padded outside, but he
didn't go far. The cold ice hurt his paws.

Spring followed winter. The fog cleared. The snow melted, except for a few patches gleaming in the sun. And Nin saw other mountains far down the trail. Two of the crew, Matt and Jake, hiked down to Mount Clay. Nin followed them. Meow! Meow! Wait for me!

Nin sniffed at little white flowers called *Diapensia*. He marched over hard boulders and soft moss and lichens.

At the top of the Great Gulf, he gazed down at a tiny lake far, far below. Nin shivered in the breeze. But he was happy to hike with Matt and Jake, exploring other peaks above the clouds. Jake let Nin drink some water from a canteen. Then they all walked back to the observatory.

The next day, on a cool and breezy morning, the Mount Washington Auto Road opened its gate. Tourists in cars drove up to the summit. Hundreds of other people rode up on the Cog Railway.

The first ones off the train were Sally, her mother and her little brother, Pete.

"Look, mom!" Sally said. "A cat. A cat on the mountain."

"A mountain lion?" asked Pete.

"No," Sally said. "Too small to be a mountain lion. And too friendly." Nin rubbed against Sally's legs and purred. "Can we take him with us?"

"He must belong to someone," said Pete.

Sally crossed her arms. "Cats don't belong to anybody. They're their own."

"But he must have a home."

"Surely not here on the mountain," said their mother. "But where?"

Nin lifted his tail and strolled inside the Sherman Adams Summit Building. Sally, Pete and their mother followed.

They followed Nin past the picnic tables. Past the gift shops full of T-shirts, postcards and little toy moose. Past the ranger's booth and the line of hikers. They walked to the end of the building. They came to the observatory.

"Here is where they study the weather," said Sally's mom.
"Hello!" said a weather observer. "Would you like a tour?"
"Let's go inside!" said Sally and Pete.

Nin walked back outside. He lay down in the sun. The wind was cool, but the sun heated the boulders. He found a nice warm rock and took a nap.

Around him visitors walked and talked and gawked at the view. Many shivered in the breeze. They were used to the warm weather below. They hadn't thought they would need jackets. But when they saw Nin, they forgot how chilly they were.

"Ooh! Look, a cat!" they said. "On a mountaintop! How strange is that?"

Nin had never seen so many people. They all liked to pet him and smile at him and tell him how handsome he was. There were plenty of laps and no other cats.

Soon the sun began to set. The tourists drove down the mountain. Nin ran back inside the observatory.

Downstairs in the kitchen, the meteorologists were talking about the weather again. "A cold front is coming through tomorrow," one person said. Nin didn't know what a cold front was. He just enjoyed the company.

  Nin jumped up onto Mark's chair and fell asleep. He had found a nice home. Here on the mountain, he decided to stay.

Appendix
Mount Washington Mascots

On April 12, 1934, five people and eight cats and kittens witnessed an incredible storm. The wind roared by at 231 miles per hour—a new world record! Meteorologists at the Mount Washington Observatory took turns going outside into the icy wind. They climbed up onto the roof and knocked rime off the scientific instruments. Oompha the cat stayed safe and warm indoors. She snuggled near the stove with two feline friends and her five baby kittens.

Blackberry

Pushka

Strawberry

Tikky

Cats have always lived at the observatory. The first cat, Tikky, had no tail. Pushka, Blackberry and their daughter, Strawberry, all liked to explore the summit when the weather was nice. A friendly calico cat named Inga even enjoyed the wintry weather. A famous picture shows Inga with ice-covered whiskers.

Inga

Jasper

A big, shy, orange cat named Jasper shared the summit with both Inga and Nin. He liked to keep the crew company but hid in a bunkroom if strangers visited the observatory. Nin showed up as a stray at the Putney School in Vermont and then came to Mount Washington a few months later. The newest cat, Marty, joined the summit crew in 2008. Like Nin, Marty likes to hike. Once he walked all the way to the Appalachian Mountain Club's Lakes of the Clouds Hut near Mount Monroe. Imagine everyone's surprise! Who expects to see a cat hiking the Appalachian Trail?

Marty

Nin still likes to sleep in the sun, dreaming about ravens and the mountain he calls home.